*Plea Of The Damned 5
Forgive Me Marti*

Plea Of The Damned 5 Forgive Me Marti

Avril Sabine

Cracked Acorn Productions
Australia

Plea Of The Damned 5: Forgive Me Marti

Published by

Cracked Acorn Productions

PO Box 1365

Gympie, Queensland 4570

Australia

978-1-925617-76-4 (Kindle)

978-1-925617-77-1 (EPUB)

978-1-925617-78-8 (Print)

Genre: Young Adult Urban/Fantasy/Paranormal

Copyright 2018 © Avril Sabine

Cover design by Caitlyn Petersen

For those who never give up, no matter the obstacles.

Plea Of The Damned

Have you ever done something and immediately wished you could undo it? Jack knows that feeling very well. He's damned, bound to haunt his old school and help students until he atones for his sins. It's the last thing he wants to do. But since the alternative is an eternity in hell, he's not about to say no.

Book 5: Forgive Me Marti

Marti's grandad always said she'd inherit his motorbike. Yet when no will is found, she's adamant there must be one and is willing to go to any lengths to find it. Or at least she was.

*

This story was written by an Australian author using Australian spelling.

Chapter One

Jack

Jack smiled as he caught sight of a cricket bat lying behind the cricket nets. Someone had obviously been in a hurry when school had ended for the September holidays, last Friday. Likely the teachers had been as keen as the students to finish up for two weeks.

He continued to walk past the bat, the smile remaining in place. He doubted he'd ever be able to look at a bat without thinking of Kobe and Xavier. It had been eleven days since they'd visited, but he'd seen them around the school during the last week before the holidays started. As always, he hadn't been able to communicate with them. He struggled not to give in to the anger that raced through him, his hand tightening into a fist as he thought back over all the students who'd wanted to talk to him. Wanted to know that he'd heard their words. It wasn't just for him that he should be able to talk to them.

Well, maybe a large part of it was for him. His anger faded away. He hated the school holidays. As lonely as it was not being able to talk to any of the students, at least during term he could see what they were up to. Could keep an eye on some of the ones he'd helped. And if previous times were anything to go by, it'd be months before he saw the angel. Months before he could talk to someone. His shoulders slumped and his steps slowed as he passed some of the classrooms. The empty classrooms. The early morning light was more than bright enough to show him exactly how empty. There weren't even kids hanging around the school grounds as some occasionally did during the holidays. Although it was fairly early. There was still a chance random kids would turn up throughout the day.

Even to himself, his thoughts sounded desperate. He didn't need the kids. They were only a means to an end. A way to atone for his sins. A sigh escaped. He wasn't fooling anyone, least of all himself. Helping the students was worse than he'd ever imagined. Figuring things out and discovering what they needed help with wasn't the real problem like he'd initially thought it would be. No, it was the brief contact and getting to know people he'd never have contact with again. The moments of company that made the days without anyone he could talk to seem lonelier.

"I hope you weren't planning on moping around all day."

Jack spun to find the angel behind him, equal amounts of annoyance and excitement rushing through him. "I don't mope." He'd been thinking, that wasn't moping.

"You do know lying is a sin."

Jack started to argue, but decided it wouldn't make a difference. For a few seconds he congratulated himself on not letting the angel goad him into an argument. "Why are you here?"

"The usual reason. Surely you didn't think there would be another."

Jack stared at the angel for a moment. Numerous questions raced through his mind, but all of them sounded like a complaint. Or at least he assumed the angel would take them that way. So soon? Already? No, not even those sounded right. "I wasn't expecting you so soon after helping Kobe."

"Are you saying this isn't a convenient time?" the angel asked.

Jack's jaw tightened. Of course the angel had to

take it the wrong way. Blasted bird. "Not at all. I was surprised. Who do you want me to help this time?" He tried not to sound too enthusiastic. But it was difficult. If they thought he enjoyed helping the students, even slightly, would they find another punishment for him? One he didn't like in the least.

"Martine. But I hear she prefers to be called Marti. Which is a shame considering what a lovely name she has."

"Does she go to this school?" He tried to think of the names of all the students. Was there one called Marti? An image came to mind of a petite girl with sandy brown hair, lots of freckles and a ready smile.

The angel inclined his head. "You'll recognise her. She'll remind you of the past."

Jack frowned. Maybe it was a different girl. Nothing about the one he'd thought of brought the past to mind. "She looks like someone from my past?"

The angel smiled, no humour in it. "That wasn't what I said. You really need to learn how to listen."

Jack breathed in slowly and deeply, determined not to let the angel get to him. Blasted bird was as far from angelic as it was possible to be. Why did he bother? "Then what do you mean? How else can she remind me of the past?"

"Have some patience, Jack. Surely I don't need to

tell you everything. I would have thought you were capable of figuring some things out for yourself by now."

Before Jack could argue with him, the angel vanished. Both his hands curled into fists and his jaw tightened on unspoken words. He kicked at a rock lying on the ground in front of him, his foot going through it and giving him no satisfaction.

"Blasted bird." He would swear the angel wasn't happy until he'd annoyed him. Were angels allowed to treat people like that? Even ghosts who had more than their share of sins to atone for. The anger faded as he contemplated asking the angel next time he saw him. It probably wouldn't be a good idea. But it was sure to be satisfying.

Chapter Two

Marti

Marti glared at her mum across the table. "No." She looked nothing like her mum, who was tall and willowy with dark brown hair cut to feather around her face. About the only thing they had in common was hazel eyes. She took after her dad's side where everyone had too many freckles, tended to be on the short side and more than a little scrawny until they became adults and gained the weight they hadn't been able to gain during childhood. They kept the freckles though. But right now, she was almost glad she didn't look like her mum. Right now she'd have preferred not to have anything to do with her. "Did you hear me? I said no."

Sally gathered her empty plate and coffee cup as she rose from the table. "It isn't an option, Martine."

She pushed the chair under the table. "Your uncle will be here to collect the bike this afternoon. Make sure you're home. He said this arve or tomorrow morning and I'm not about to get out of bed early on a Saturday morning after working all week."

Marti pushed the chair back, following her mum to the sink. "It's my bike. Grandad left it to me. We built it together."

"I'm not arguing with you about this. There was no will so you don't get to keep it."

"Grandad always said it would go to me. That he put it in his will. We just have to find it." Marti stepped in front of Sally when she tried to leave the kitchen.

"I don't have time for this. I need to get ready for work."

"Mum-"

"No. There is no will. It was probably yet one more thing he put off until it was too late." Sally stepped around Marti.

"You never wanted me to have the bike or you'd help me fight for it. And help look for the will." She glared at her mum's back.

Sally stopped at the doorway, looking over her shoulder. "Hector and I are divorced so it has nothing to do with me anymore."

"Just because you and Dad are divorced doesn't mean I'm no longer a part of his family."

"Enough." Sally held up a hand when Marti started to speak again. "I mean it. The bike goes today."

"Mum-"

"Today. If it's here when I get home you're grounded for the rest of the year." Sally strode out of sight.

Marti glared at the empty doorway. It wasn't fair. The bike was meant to be hers. Her grandad had promised. Had been promising her since she was ten and they'd begun to rebuild it together. She'd been the first one he'd taken for a ride, the first one to see it finished, the first one to offer to help when it needed a service. It had been their thing. Something only the two of them had liked to do.

She closed her eyes, clenching her teeth together as she fought against the tears that wanted to spill. There was no way she was about to let her uncle get hold of the bike. He'd only sell it. Had thought it a waste of money. Drawing in a shaky breath, she opened her eyes and returned to her bedroom, picking up her phone off the bedside cabinet where she'd left it since she wasn't allowed to have it at the table.

She stared at the screen. There was no one she could call. It was nearly the end of the first week of the September school holidays and no one was about. Not her best friend, not her boyfriend and none of the kids she occasionally hung out with. There was no one she could ask for help. Nowhere she could hide the bike. She lowered her hand, slipping her phone into a pocket of her jeans. Yet she couldn't let Gordon take the bike. It'd be like losing the last link to her grandad.

"Martine! I'm leaving now."

She turned to face the bedroom door she'd left open as she heard Sally's voice come closer.

Sally stopped in the doorway. "I'll see you at five-thirty. Why not get your assignments done while you're waiting for your uncle to turn up. No point leaving them until the last minute. School will be back in again before you know it."

She stared at Sally. School. It would be empty for a bit over a week. Enough time to find a way to search her grandad's house. She still had the key he'd given her for when she randomly visited him.

"Well?"

For a moment she forgot what Sally had said, shrugging in answer, eventually nodding when Sally's lips pressed tightly together. "See you this arve."

Sally sighed. "It won't bring him back. Nothing will."

"Like you care that he died."

Sally opened her mouth, closing it and slowly shaking her head, walking away without saying a word.

Her mum might be right and the bike wouldn't bring him back, but it helped. The smells, the sound of the engine, the familiar feel of the various parts when she ran her hands over them, they all brought back vivid memories. And she didn't want to risk losing a single memory.

Grabbing the backpack she preferred to use instead of a handbag, she hurried to the front of the house, peering through the lounge room window at Sally's car disappearing down the street. She waited several minutes before she ran to the garage, in case Sally had forgotten something. Like always, she paused in the doorway, drinking in the sight of the 1953 Royal Enfield Bullet. A smile formed and she could almost see her grandad polishing the silver fuel tank with his full head of white hair and the many freckles scattered across his face, unfaded. In the past handful of years he'd lost the weight he'd carried most of his adult life, his frame becoming more like the scrawny one of his youth. Yet he'd never lost his exuberance for life or the pleasure he'd gained from working on his bike. Even after it had been completely rebuilt.

She closed the door behind her as she meandered towards the bike, the smile remaining in place as she ran her hand over the fuel tank. It had been the first bike he'd ever owned. Not this particular one. That one had been wrecked by Gordon when he was eighteen. No, this one he'd searched years for, finally finding one that had needed a lot of attention. They'd worked on it together. She knew every single part of the bike as well as her grandad had known it. They'd stripped it down and put it back together numerous times.

"I won't let him get it, Grandad." The words were a whisper. He hadn't wanted Gordon to wreck a second one. Had never let him borrow this one. Not that Gordon had been allowed to borrow the first one. "I know you had a will. You told me several times. Said you'd made sure he couldn't get his hands on it." She breathed in deeply, the smell of the bike so familiar.

Chapter Three

Marti

Straightening her shoulders, Marti took a deep breath before she strode to the garage door and pushed it up, wincing at the sound. It was a good thing Sally wasn't home. Not with the amount of noise the roller door made. Once the bike was outside, on the driveway, the central stand down, she closed and locked the roller door, returning her bunch of keys to her backpack. A glance around showed no one was nearby. The neighbouring houses were quiet and the traffic driving past was light. She doubted anyone was paying her any attention.

Her stomach turned and she tried to ignore the sensation. It wasn't like Gordon had left her any choice. Or Sally. It was her bike. Her grandad had wanted her to have it. Hadn't believed anyone else would look after it the way he had.

It took her fifteen minutes to reach the school and she wheeled the bike in the front gate, glancing over her shoulder. Something she hadn't been able to stop doing the entire walk. Nor had she dared ride the bike since she didn't have a license. It was something she planned to get. After she went for her car license when she turned seventeen. Her arms and legs ached from pushing the bike the entire way. At least there'd been no steep hills between her place and the school to push it up.

Looking around, she saw no one. The place was deserted. Now all she had to do was figure out where to stash the bike. Surely there was somewhere out of the way where it'd be safe until she could find the will. Both Hector and Gordon had said there was no will, but she knew better. They'd obviously not looked properly.

She headed to the left, slowing when she saw a young man come around the corner of a building, freezing when he caught sight of her. He wore jeans and a black leather jacket, a white t-shirt under it, and his dark hair was styled in a fashion that probably hadn't been popular since the sixties. When he laughed, the sound ringing out, she came to a stop, scanning the area for an escape. She wasn't about to save the bike from Gordon to let it fall into the hands of some crazy guy.

He strode towards her, a smile remaining in place.

She turned the handlebars, planning to head in a different direction. He acted like he knew her and she'd never seen him before in her life.

"Martine. Marti. Wait."

She looked over her shoulder, frowning. He knew her? She looked him up and down as he continued to stride towards her. He didn't seem at all familiar.

He reached her side, his dark eyes fixed on the bike. "The blasted bird was right. You do remind me of the past. Or at least your bike does." He started to reach for it, lowering his hand as his smile faded. "I haven't seen an Enfield in decades."

She eyed him up and down again. "Decades." Just her luck to run into some crazy person. She was beginning to think she had the worst luck ever.

He held out a hand. "I'm Jack Richards."

She didn't take his hand. She kept walking, her hands tightening on the handlebars as she hoped he'd get the message and leave her alone. Maybe this wasn't the place to hide the bike. But where else could she take it? She doubted she'd be able to take it much further with how her arms and legs ached.

Jack lowered his hand. "I'm here to help you."

This time she did stop, facing him as she kept hold of the bike, putting the stand down so she didn't risk dropping it with how badly her body ached. "You what?" She glanced around the school grounds. "Is Uncle Gordon here?" Another glance around showed the place was empty, other than the two of them. "He's not having it. You can tell him I said that."

"I don't know your uncle. I'm not here to take your bike. I'm here to help." Jack sighed heavily. "This is the part I always hate."

She slowly shook her head, putting the stand up and beginning to push it again. She should know better than to talk to some stranger. There wasn't time. She needed to find somewhere to hide the bike. The will wasn't going to miraculously appear in front of her.

"I'm a ghost. Died in 1963 on my eighteenth birthday and now I'm stuck here, helping students so I can atone for my sins."

Glancing over her shoulder, she opened her mouth to ask him a question, slowly shaking her head again. She wasn't about to get caught up in his problems. She had enough of her own. He was obviously in need of some serious help.

Jack picked up his pace, getting ahead of her to stand directly in front of her. "Marti-"

"Out of the way." She kept going, expecting him to move. The bike went through his figure, stopping partway through him when her arm connected with his body. She froze, her mouth hanging open as she looked from his face to the bike parked in his body. "You…" She closed her eyes, shaking her head once more. "No." Opening her eyes she found he hadn't moved. "Ghosts don't exist."

"So people keep telling me."

"But-" Again her gaze was drawn to the bike. "How-" She met his dark eyes. "What-" Not a single sentence fully formed. Then it struck her and she breathed in sharply. "You're here to help me?"

Jack nodded.

"Did my grandad send you?"

"No."

"Are you sure?"

"Yeah."

"Can I talk to him through you? To his spirit or something."

"What do you think I am? A Ouija board?"

"You said you're here to help."

"And there's the other part I hate." Jack met her

gaze. "The help you need isn't always the help you want."

Chapter Four

Marti

"I should have known there'd be a catch," Marti muttered. "Get out of the way. I need to find somewhere to hide my bike. I have other things to do." Like find the will and get home before her mum finished work.

"Why do you need to hide it?" Jack glanced down at the bike.

"My grandad left it to me."

"That doesn't explain why you need to hide it."

Her gaze travelled the length of the bike, or at least the length of it that wasn't hidden by Jack. She really needed to find somewhere to hide it before she dropped it. Her arms were starting to shake from the effort of holding it upright. "No one can find his will and without it, they're not about to let me keep it. Uncle Gordon because he's determined to sell everything and my parents because they don't want me to have it. They think it's too dangerous." She winced when her gaze returned to Jack. "Can you move? Don't you know how disturbing that is?" She nodded to where the bike disappeared into his body.

Jack chuckled, stepping to the side with a shrug. "You get used to it."

"Not likely." She started to move forward.

"You can hide it in the groundsman's shed." He glanced in the direction of the treed area that she'd been heading towards before he'd arrived. "I can unlock it for you. Without setting off the alarm."

"Without… oh." She hadn't thought about the alarm. There was obviously quite a few things she hadn't thought about. How was she meant to figure out what to do when she'd never done anything like this before?

Jack gestured in the direction of the groundsman's shed. "Want me to unlock it for you?"

"Do the groundsmen work during the holidays?"

"Not on the weekend. And not all the time. At the earliest, they'll be here Monday morning. They were here yesterday and one asked if the other had plans for their long weekend. There's always a chance they won't work again until Tuesday."

She stopped again, looking from the direction she'd been walking in to the direction of the groundsman's shed that wasn't visible from where she stood. "Okay. Unlock it for me." She kept glancing at Jack as she walked beside him, trying to decide how to word her question.

"Is something wrong?"

"Yes. I mean, no. I–" She broke off her babbling. "How did you end up a ghost?"

"I was stabbed."

"Oh. Did they catch the person who killed you?"

Jack didn't answer immediately. "Don't feel sympathy for me. I deserved it."

She stopped once more, putting the stand down to give her arms a rest as she stared at him. "You deserved being stabbed?"

Jack chuckled. "I'd like to say no, but I don't think there are many who'd agree with me."

She started to ask him what he'd done to deserve being stabbed, but another thought occurred to her. "Can you ask my grandad a question for me? When you go to wherever ghosts or spirits go."

"I don't go anywhere. This is it." He made a sweeping gesture.

"Do you think my grandad is stuck somewhere?"

"What was he like?"

"The best grandad ever."

"Then I doubt it. This is a special kind of hell they keep for the worst of sinners."

She frowned. "You're in hell?" She glanced around the school grounds. She wasn't overly fond of school, but she wouldn't have exactly called it hell.

"No, but I will end up there if I don't atone for my sins."

"What kind of sins?"

Jack remained silent for a moment. "Didn't you say you had other plans for the day?"

She grinned. "There's that many?"

Jack didn't return her smile. "Yes."

"Oh." Her smile faded and she glanced over her shoulder, wondering if she should remain where she was.

"You're safe."

She met his gaze, seeing something deep in his eyes. Regret? Sorrow? She wasn't sure and didn't know if she should ask. "Are you sure you can't talk to my grandad?"

"The only ones I can talk to is an angel and whoever I'm helping. Not that I've helped many."

Hope rose. Surely angels could talk to whoever they wanted. Including someone who'd died eight months ago. "Can you ask the angel to talk to my grandad?"

"No."

"Why not?"

"He isn't interested in anything I have to say, only telling me who I should help next and pointing out my failings. Which he probably believes are numerous."

She was surprised by the bitterness in his tone. "What about the people you've helped. Can they see other ghosts? Talk to the dead?"

"You're the only one I can currently talk to."

Once again she found herself staring at him open-mouthed. Closing her mouth, she felt an urge to cry. She rested a hand on his shoulder. "I'm sorry."

"Why are you sorry?"

"That I can't spend the rest of the afternoon with you. I need to find my grandad's will." It wasn't like she'd have much time to find it. Not after her mum found out what she'd done. And Gordon was sure to tell her.

Jack again stared silently at her. "Why would you think you need to spend the afternoon with me?"

"Because you're alone." She couldn't imagine anything worse. Time alone was good, but only getting to talk to someone rarely, that would be terrible.

Again Jack remained silent before he spoke. "You're not here for my benefit. I'm here to help you."

She smiled. "Who's to say it isn't both?"

"Because I don't deserve it to be both." He looked away from her. "I'll unlock the shed for you."

Chapter Five

Marti

Marti put the stand up and followed Jack, wanting to ask what he'd done that was so bad. But she didn't. His tone made her think he'd rather not say. Ahead of her, Jack walked through the door of the groundsman's shed and it swung open. She pushed the bike inside, glancing around the dim and cluttered interior, very little light reaching the far side of the shed. "Are you sure it'll be okay in here?" She put the stand down, then rubbed at her aching arms.

"I'll keep an eye on it." Jack stood in front of the bike, his gaze fixed on it.

She smiled. His expression reminded her of the one her grandad had often worn when he'd looked at it. "You owned one."

Jack nodded. "Yeah. Back in the sixties. She was a sweet ride."

She took a step backwards, still needing to find the will. "You'll be here when I return?" She doubted she could leave the bike here without checking on it at least a couple of times.

He nodded to a wardrobe in the far corner of the shed. "There's a gap between it and the wall, a space behind it where I sometimes hang out."

"Okay. I'll be back later. I need to find my grandad's will." She started for the door.

Jack stopped her, a hand on her shoulder. "I don't think that's a good idea."

"Why not? How else am I going to prove the bike belongs to me?"

"Some things aren't worth the risk."

"The bike is. Grandad wanted me to have it. No one else. Me."

"Is it worth your life?"

She started to ask him what he meant. Shaking her head, she stepped away from him, dislodging his hand from her shoulder. "You obviously spend too much time on your own. That was a terrible joke."

"It wasn't a joke."

She backed away from him, ignoring the unsettling feeling his words caused. "Not funny, Jack.

Not funny at all." She broke into a run, heading for the fence and clambering over it. Maybe she should have asked him about his sins. He was a ghost and she'd seen more than enough horror movies to know that they were often the problem. The one that took out the characters one by one. A shiver ran through her, a cold chill following it.

Slowing to a walk, she rubbed her arms. It was a warm day, yet it didn't feel that way to her. She scanned the area. Were there other ghosts? Would she be able to see them if there was? She had no idea and didn't know how she could find a reliable source of information.

It took twenty minutes to reach her grandad's house. Not long enough for her to answer the question that continued to run through her mind. Pushing aside thoughts of ghosts, crazy or otherwise, she took out her keys and unlocked the front door of the unpainted Besser block house. The grass was in need of mowing and the two garden beds across the front of the house were filled with dead plants. It made her heart ache to see them. Didn't anyone care about the place now he was gone?

She'd offered to take care of things, but Sally had argued about her spending time here alone and Gordon had been adamant that no one should be in the house without him there too. Hector included. Which was why it was taking so long to sort out the estate. Everything had to be argued over. She'd heard plenty of complaints from Hector about it.

Locking the door behind her, Marti froze. Where was the lounge suite with the worn, comfy chair her grandad had often fallen asleep in when they'd watched the television together? The buffet that had belonged to her grandma and had been filled with fancy glasses no one used. Framed photos of places and people from long ago had been scattered across the top of it, a couple of modern ones amongst them. Even the old television, nothing like the flat screens her parents owned, was gone.

There was a stale smell to the empty room and she blinked back tears, holding herself still until she was able to force them away. Was there anything left? She walked unsteadily across the room, opening the closed door that led to the main bedroom. Pain arrowed through her and she clung to the doorframe. Nothing. No furniture, no unmade bed and no cane armchair in the corner of the room. She stared at the corner but it remained empty, the armchair filled with odds and ends and the clothes he'd changed out of to work on the bike no longer there.

Her grip tightened on the door frame. It was like

someone was erasing him from the house, one room at a time. She took a step back, glancing at the front door, tempted to flee. She remained where she was, breathing heavily, feeling like she'd run a race, in the lead the entire way only to lose at the end.

There had to be something. She ran to the kitchen, nearly running into the timber table, four matching chairs pushed in around it, paper stacked in neat piles across the top. She clutched the back of the closest chair, giddiness washing over her. They hadn't completely erased him from the house yet.

She started to sag against the chair. A sound startled her and had her facing the fridge. She laughed at herself when she realised it was the motor kicking in. Swinging the fridge door open, she frowned. Not a single item in there had belonged to her grandad. There was a six-pack of Gordon's favourite beer, a jar of stuffed olives, a half a loaf of bread, Vegemite and butter. Was Gordon staying here? He wasn't meant to be here without Hector. That had been the deal they'd struck.

Closing the fridge door, she faced the piles of paper on the table, daunted by the amount of them. It was going to take a while. Straightening her shoulders, she returned to the table, starting on the first stack, checking through every single piece of paper, keeping them in order in case there was some method to what looked like random piles.

After a few hours, she began to think it was an impossible task. How could any one person accumulate so many pieces of paper? Needing a break and starving since it was lunchtime, she made herself a sandwich, spreading it only with butter. She didn't care how un-Australian it made her, but she didn't like Vegemite. Not feeling up to staring at the piles she still had to check through, Marti took out her keys and entered the laundry, unlocking the deadbolt on the back door. She took the keys out of the lock, keeping them with her when she stepped into the backyard. She'd learned the hard way that there was no getting inside if the door was blown shut and you had no keys with you.

A smile formed. Her and her grandad had learned the hard way. She'd gone inside for a drink and had left the keys on the table, not taking them back outside with her. They'd been washing the bike in the backyard, under the shade of the tree partway along the side fence. A gust of wind had slammed the door shut and they'd had to break into the house.

His words rang in her mind along with the image of him helping her climb through the bathroom window. 'Lucky you're such a little thing.' She'd smiled and corrected him. Telling him she was scrawny. 'No. Just the perfect size.' His words had made her smile widen.

Chapter Six

Marti

Marti wandered towards the back fence and the garden shed, eating the sandwich. A dog barked at her from behind the fence. "Oh, be quiet." He barked again. She looked around the yard. It was in worse shape than the front. Weeds were growing in the once tidy lawn and there were sticks and leaves scattered beneath the tree. Her grandad had paid someone to come in every month to take care of the lawn, only worrying about watering the gardens out the front. He'd be sad to see the state it was in.

Finished the last mouthful, she returned inside, reluctantly starting on the last few piles. She didn't find it. Stretching as she rose from the chair, she surveyed the kitchen. The will hadn't been in any of the piles of paper. She'd been so certain she'd find it.

Opening several of the kitchen cupboards, she found nothing. They were empty. Was this it? The table of paper and a fridge with food that hadn't belonged to her grandad? She opened the bathroom door. Another empty room. Even the shower curtain had been taken down.

Rushing to the final door she hadn't opened she stood staring at it, afraid to open it and see what was inside. What if it was empty too? How would she find the will? She knew there was one. But she was rapidly running out of places to look. Tightening her grip on the handle, she held her breath as she turned the knob, pushing the door open. She let out her breath in a rush of air. The spare room was as full of clutter as always. A desk buried under odds and ends, including motorbike parts, an ironing board that had been turned into a place to store items and probably hadn't been used for its actual purpose for several years, a chest of drawers with two broken handles that were meant to be fixed one day, a few boxes stacked along one wall with a film of dust across them and a basket of laundry needing to be folded. She could clearly see him walking into the room, hands on his hips as he surveyed the mess. With a shrug, he always turned to her with a smile. 'It can wait till later. How about a ride?'

She'd always agreed. Every single time.

Crossing the room, she picked up a broken photo frame off the ironing board, staring at the photograph. Tears formed. This time she let them fall as she ran a finger along the edge of the frame. This was how she always saw him. A large man who was a little on the short side, with a large laugh, a smile always in place and blue eyes filled with excitement. One hand rested on the seat of his bike and his arm was draped around her shoulders. The two of them and the bike was all that was in the picture. The scenery behind them a blur, making them stand out sharply against it. She remembered the day it had been taken. Her grandma had taken the photo, teasing him about taking a photo of him with the two loves of his life. He'd teased her back and somehow she'd ended up taking a photo of her grandparents next to the bike. It had been out of focus, but her grandad had put it in a frame and it had sat on the top of the buffet with this one until the wind had knocked this one over and it had remained in the spare room waiting to be fixed.

But things tended not to be fixed when they ended up in the spare room. The only thing that he'd ever got around to fixing was the bike. Brushing away tears, Marti returned to the kitchen and shoved the photo frame in her backpack. She doubted Gordon would want it and Hector probably didn't care what happened to the photo. He'd hated the bike. Like Gordon, he'd thought it a waste of time and money.

A sound had her rising to her feet and she realised it was the sound of the front door opening. Slinging her backpack into place, she started for the back door she'd left open.

"What are you doing here?"

She spun to face Gordon, remaining in the doorway of the laundry.

"You shouldn't be here."

She glared at Gordon. "It's not just your place. It's Dad's place too."

"It won't be anyone's place soon. It's being sold to pay out the loan the old man had on the place."

Shock raced through her. "You're selling it? You're selling grandad's house?"

"What did you think we were going to do? Set it up as a shrine to him?"

Her jaw tightened, her teeth gritted together against the words that wanted to spill. But it'd only lead to harsher comments from Gordon.

"Sally said you'd be at home. With the bike. I knocked on the door for ages."

She tried not to smile. It was difficult. The image of

him impatiently demanding someone open the door filled her mind. It was a rather satisfying thought.

"Where is it?" Gordon demanded.

"It's mine. Grandad left it to me."

"There's no will. Which means it's not yours. It belongs to the old man's heirs." He pointed a finger at her. "Which isn't you."

"Dad is an-"

"Hector agreed to sell it for what we can get. The only thing of value the old man had was that bike. What did you do with it? He wasted too much money on it. More than it's worth. We'll be lucky to get six grand for it."

"You're not selling it. Grandad said it was mine."

He took a step towards her. "You are-"

"Gordon. What's taking you?" A deep voice called from the front of the house.

"I told you to wait outside."

The man who stepped into the kitchen towered over Gordon and was as wide as him. Yet from the way his clothes moulded across his chest, unlike Gordon, it was all muscle. She took a step backwards, wanting to check the distance between her and the door, yet unable to take her gaze from the newcomer.

"And I told you-" He broke off when he caught sight of Marti. "Is that the girl? That your niece?"

"I'll find the bike, Warren. She'll tell me where it is."

"She better."

A shiver ran through her at the tone he used, panic on its heels. Spinning, she ran for the back door, slamming it shut behind her, ignoring their yells to return. Pausing under the tree, she grabbed three sticks before continuing towards the back fence. She threw a stick at the fence, the noise causing the dog to bark. The other two sticks were thrown over the fence the third one further than the second.

Her fingers fumbled on the handle of the garden shed, turning the lever and only opening the door enough to slip inside. She tried not to think about what might be inside the shed with her as she closed the door, shutting out most of the light. A bit of light crept in around the edges of the door and where the corrugated aluminium walls met the roof.

Chapter Seven

Marti

Taking out her phone, Marti turned on the flashlight app, shining the light across the jumble of items. The lawnmower had been left near the door, the grass not washed off like it usually was. She shined the light over the rest of the contents of the shed, all the time listening for pursuit. The neighbour's dog continued to bark, but everything else was silent. She tucked herself in behind a metal rubbish bin that hadn't been used for years, holding back a scream when she ran into a cobweb.

Frantically checking herself over for spiders, she froze when she heard her name called. Gordon called again, his voice coming closer. She turned off the flashlight app, trying not to think about the cobweb that clung to her face and hands.

"She's gone over the fence," Gordon said.

Marti held her breath, he sounded like he was right outside.

"With that dog?"

"Yeah," Gordon said. "He barks a lot, but doesn't bite."

"You said this would be simple. That you'd have the bike to us before the end of the day."

"It is simple and the day's not over yet. Hector is happy to take six for the bike. And the balance of what it's worth can be taken from the money I owe. Along with my share of the six. Then that'll be most of my debt paid off. It won't take us much longer to finish clearing out the house and then that can go up for sale. I'll be paid out in no time."

"You better be right." There was a clear warning in Warren's tone.

Marti stared at the outline of the door. Gordon was obviously lying to one of them about the value of the house. He'd told her the only thing of value had been the bike. She had a feeling it was Warren who was being lied to. And she doubted it'd be good when he learned the truth.

Gordon yelled at the dog to be quiet, threatening him with dire consequences. The only difference it made was to make him bark louder.

Something striking the wall of the shed had Marti shrinking further back behind the metal bin. A shiver went through her as cobwebs brushed against her cheek. She pressed a hand over her mouth to prevent a scream from escaping.

"She could have gone in here," Warren said.

The door swung open and Gordon peered inside.

Marti held her breath, remaining as still as possible and hoping the shadows hid her from view. She could barely see Gordon from where she crouched behind the bin. Would he be able to see her?

"Told you. She jumped the fence. Didn't you hear the dog carrying on worse than usual?" Gordon slammed the door shut.

"You better find her."

"She's sixteen. She'll go home before her mum finishes work or she's going to be grounded." Gordon chuckled. "In fact, I'm going to insist she's grounded after all the trouble she's caused." Gordon's voice sounded like it was a little further away from the shed.

Marti came out from behind the bin slightly, finally able to brush the cobwebs away from her face.

"I'll wait for her there and call you when I find out where the bike is," Gordon said.

"I'm going with you. The boss said not to let you

out of my sight until you pay up. That if you try and run I'm to make it impossible for you to do so."

She'd started to rise to her feet, stopping when she heard them arguing, remaining in the backyard. Sighing, she sat down on the floor, her calves aching from crouching so long and probably from how far she'd pushed the bike earlier. There was no way she could go home. Not until after her mum was there. She sent a message.

Can I go to the movies?

It took a few minutes for her mum to answer and still Gordon and Warren continued to argue outside. *What time will you be home?*

Eight. Actually, eight-thirty. We'll have takeaway for dinner. She hoped her mum didn't ask who 'we' was since she couldn't think of a single suitable name to give.

Make sure you're home by eight-thirty at the latest.

Okay. She stared at her phone, but it remained dark, no further messages coming through. Her gaze was drawn to the door and she sighed. How long were they going to stand out there arguing?

Not knowing what else to do, and trying to take her mind off the cobwebs nearby that might contain spiders, she opened a browser on her phone. She did a search on Jack Richards, using the name of her school to help since it seemed to be a common name. The first result was a blog post by an anonymous blogger who only had the one post. She read it over, surprised to find it was about Jack. There was an old photograph of him along with numerous newspaper articles, some of which had been poorly scanned. The blogger talked about Jack's life. Losing his mum, being stabbed by his girlfriend, Rose, and him shooting her and her new boyfriend. She read over the last couple of lines of the blog post.

'I like to think he's sorry and wants to atone for his mistakes. That he somehow has the chance to atone. That he regrets that one moment he can't take back and doesn't think he can ever be forgiven for it. Some people, even though they come into your life for such a short period of time make a greater impact than those you've known forever.'

She read the words over again. Was it written by one of the students he'd helped? She looked at the comments on the post, scrolling past the ones pointing out Jack was dead and long gone. Should she ask? She didn't know. It wasn't like anyone had come straight out and said Jack was a ghost. She scrolled through more of the comments, stopping at one from someone asking the blogger if they'd known Jack during his life.

'You might say I knew him in his death.'

It had to be one of the students he'd helped. She was almost certain of it. She started to type in a reply, realising it was quiet outside. Locking her phone screen, she slipped it back into her pocket, getting to her feet. Her hand hovered above the door handle, eventually closing around the lever and slowly turning it.

She opened the door a crack, scanning the backyard. As far as she could tell, it was empty. She opened the door further. No one. Even the dog was quiet. Several cautious steps gave her a better view of the backyard. Still no one.

Closing the shed door, she started towards the house, changing her mind and jumping the fence instead. She wasn't about to risk running into Gordon and Warren. That seemed like a really bad idea. Especially running into Warren.

Chapter Eight

Marti

The dog barked and jumped around Marti as she made her way to the side gate of the yard, trying to avoid being licked and jumped on. "Settle down." Her words only encouraged him to jump around her more enthusiastically. Reaching the gate, she struggled to leave without letting him escape. Finally closing the gate behind herself, she glared at the dog. "You need to learn some manners."

A glance around showed she was alone and she strode down the street, returning to school. Jack met her before she could enter the groundsman's shed and she looked past him at the building. "There are no cobwebs in the shed, are there?" She didn't think she could face more cobwebs today. Not after being forced to sit in them for so long.

Jack shrugged. "There are some in your hair."

She brushed at her hair, having thought she'd got rid of all the cobwebs during the walk to her school, trying to tell herself that there couldn't be any spiders or she would have felt them. "No one found my bike?"

"No. Did you find the will?"

She shook her head, following Jack inside, taking out her phone to use the flashlight app. When Jack continued to the far corner, walking through a wardrobe, she followed, turning sideways to enter the space behind the wardrobe. "How did you set up this area?" Her gaze was drawn from a picture of Rose hanging on the wall, that she recognised from the blog post, to a cushion on the floor and a bat propped up in the corner. There was a battery-powered lantern that she turned on so she didn't have to waste her phone charge by using the flashlight app.

"Those I've helped did most of it."

She sat on the cushion after dusting off her jeans. "I think I found one of them online."

Jack frowned, sitting beside her, drawing his knee up to rest his arm on it. "Found who online?"

"One of the students you helped." She explained about the blogger. "Do you know who it is?"

Jack smiled. "I think so."

"Can I contact them?"

He shrugged. "I wouldn't have a clue. That blasted bird tells me nothing."

"Oh." She put her phone away, not sure what to say. "How do you normally help people?"

"By giving them advice that they ignore."

She chuckled.

"I'm serious."

Her smile half faded. "You're-" She broke off. He had to be joking. "Why are you the one helping?"

"You know the answer to that question. It was in the blog post you told me about. It's this or hell."

"You don't want to help?" She met his dark gaze, waiting for an answer she began to think wasn't going to come.

"Not at first."

"But you do now?"

A wry smile made a fleeting appearance. "I guess I'm more lame than I thought."

She laughed, sobering before she spoke again. "How am I going to find my grandad's will?"

"What happened while you were gone?"

She told him everything. Including her encounter with Gordon and Warren.

"Forget about it. As great as that bike is, it's not

worth your life. Would your grandad want you killed in an effort to keep it?"

"It's mine. Why should I let them get away with it?"

"You're going to ignore me, aren't you?"

"Not if you come up with a decent suggestion."

"Decent doesn't mean you'll be happy with it."

"Okay. A decent suggestion I'll be happy with. My bike. Grandad and I did that bike up together. I'm not going to let Uncle Gordon get rid of it to pay off some debt."

Jack stared at her, frowning.

"What's wrong?"

"Who is he in debt to and why? Have you considered you don't have enough information to make any decisions about what you should be doing? For all you know, he could be in debt to someone who'd kill both of you and dump your bodies in the Brisbane River."

A shudder ran through her. "Uncle Gordon doesn't know people like that."

"You sure?"

She started to say yes, but something stopped her. It couldn't be possible. Maybe people like that existed in her city, but surely she didn't know a single person who associated with any of them. She glanced at the picture of Rose, wanting to change the subject. "What was she like? Your girlfriend."

Jack's gaze was drawn to the picture. "It was a long time ago."

"Does that mean you've forgotten?"

Jack met her gaze. "Never. Some people are impossible to forget. Even if you have no reminders of them." He paused a moment. "Including a bike."

A sigh escaped. So much for changing the topic. "I'm going to find somewhere to buy something to eat. It's been a long day and other than breakfast I've only had a piece of buttered bread. I'm starving." She turned on her flashlight app before she turned off the lantern, getting to her feet. "I'll be back soon." After she'd come up with a plan.

On her way to the door, she stopped at the bike to run one hand across the seat. Jack was wrong. It wasn't just about remembering her grandad. It was about fighting to fulfil his last wish.

It was dark when she returned and Jack met her at the front entrance as she strode onto the school grounds. She was still no closer to a plan and had begun to think she'd never come up with one. There were questions she wanted to ask Jack, but she really didn't want the conversation to return to her problems so she remained silent. She meandered through the school grounds, slowly making her way towards the groundsman's shed, eventually needing to use the flashlight app to find her way. A couple of times she glanced at Jack, but he remained as silent as she did.

When she was seated in the area behind the wardrobe, she tried to think of something to fill the uncomfortable silence. In the end, she asked one of the questions that had been bothering her. "How long did you miss her?" She glanced at the picture of Rose.

"I still miss her."

"Oh."

"It's not something you stop doing. It's something you learn to live with." He paused a moment. "How long since your grandad died?"

"Eight months." She turned on the battery-powered lantern, fiddling with it.

Jack inclined his head, once again sitting beside the cushion with his leg drawn up and his arm resting on his knee. "Keeping the bike won't bring him back."

"I know." She brought up the blog post again scrolling through the comments, asking Jack if he wanted to see some of them. He looked over her shoulder as she continued to scroll, occasionally asking her to keep the page still.

Chapter Nine

Marti

When a call came through from her mum, Marti sent it to message bank and put a temporary block on all incoming calls. The only reason her mum would be calling her while she was supposedly watching a movie was because Gordon had complained about her not being there so he could pick up the bike.

The conversation finally turned to other things and she found herself talking about music and bikes. Mostly bikes. She showed him images on her phone of the various models, like hers, that people had restored. She grinned at his comments. "You're definitely old school. There's nothing wrong with making a few changes. I'm not saying neon paint jobs or anything. But it doesn't have to be factory perfect."

The alarm on her phone went off, interrupting

Jack who'd been arguing her statement. "What's the alarm for?" He gestured to the phone.

She turned on the flashlight app before turning off the lantern. "I have to head home. Mum won't be impressed if I'm late." She'd set the alarm earlier when she'd been getting something to eat, along with checking what movies were on in case her mum asked what she'd seen. She'd also checked the movie rating and read a few spoilers for it.

Jack followed her outside. "I can't leave the school grounds. If you want my help, you need to stay here."

"I can't stay here, Jack." She briefly rested a hand against his arm. "Thanks for keeping me company and thank you for somewhere to stash my bike until I can find the will." Not that she knew how she was going to return to her grandad's house without being caught by Gordon and Warren.

"I thought you'd already looked for it."

"I didn't get a chance to search the spare room."

"You're out of your tree. Going back there alone is going to get you killed."

She refused to let his words bother her. "I will find it. I'm not about to let Uncle Gordon get away with this."

"What if he has burned it? From what you said

he seems pretty confident that there's no will. That might be because he's made sure there isn't one."

Shock raced through her and she found herself speechless, opening and closing her mouth several times. She shook her head as she backed away. "No. He couldn't. That's…" Surely Jack was wrong. Gordon couldn't have destroyed his own father's will. "I-" She broke off, trying to gather her thoughts. "I have to go." She hurried away, unable to outpace the thoughts Jack had put in her head. How could she prove it was her bike if Gordon had destroyed the will?

In an effort to take her mind off such thoughts, she tried to come up with a reason why she was a mess. She thought of and discarded several excuses before she settled on one that sounded logical.

Drawing nearer to home, she decided to sneak in from the back neighbour's yard in case Gordon and Warren were watching the house. None of the neighbours had dogs, a few had cats, but nothing that would make a lot of noise and warn anyone she was about. Turning off her flashlight app, she slipped her phone into her pocket before clambering over the back fence. The backyard was familiar enough she was able to cross it in the dark, reaching the back door to find it unlocked. Slipping inside, she locked it.

Her mum was in the lounge room and looked up from the television as she entered. "What have you done to yourself? You're a mess. Are those cobwebs on your jeans? Where did you go? I thought you were going to the movies."

Marti held up a hand. "Give me a break. How am I meant to answer anything if you keep firing questions at me?"

"Well?"

"I ran into a spider's web and tripped over when I was trying to get away from it."

"And the movie?"

She shrugged. "It was all right."

"I tried to ring you earlier."

She shrugged again. "I had my phone turned off so I didn't disturb anyone. I guess I forgot to turn it back on." She tried to remain calm. "Were you ringing for anything important?"

"Gordon was here."

She remained silent. There wasn't much she could say. Not without a will to prove the bike belonged to her.

"What did you do with his bike?"

"It's not his bike."

Sally rose to her feet, meeting Marti's gaze. "You

will collect the bike from wherever you put it and hand it over to Gordon tomorrow afternoon."

"Is that what he demanded?" Maybe she'd overreacted by sneaking in the back door.

"He wanted it tonight. I told him to come back tomorrow." Sally pointed a finger at her. "And I don't want another argument on the topic. Have a shower and get ready for bed."

Marti escaped to her room, grabbing clothes and heading to the bathroom to have a shower. She put on another pair of jeans and a t-shirt since she wasn't ready for bed. She was wide awake. Sitting at her desk, she turned her computer on and returned to the blog post. Jack hadn't exactly said not to contact anyone. Hands resting on the keyboard, she alternated between deciding she'd ask them and worried it would get Jack in trouble.

Eventually, she typed a message. 'If you had the chance to say one thing to Jack, what would it be?' She stared at her words. Was it too late to delete them? Could they be deleted now she'd posted them?

She was about to close the page when a reply appeared. 'He's dead. Why would the original poster want to say anything to him?'

She typed in another message, all the while telling

herself not to reply to the troll. 'Obviously you've never lost anyone.'

Another reply appeared and she nearly didn't bother reading it, expecting it to be from the troll. 'That he manages to atone for his sins. He might not be able to change the past, but he can make a difference in the future for so many others.' It was rapidly followed by two more replies. 'I'll never forget you.' 'I often find myself walking past the groundsman's shed wondering if you would hear me if I said hello.'

Excitement raced through her. All three posters were anonymous. The troll had been a mixture of numbers and letters. She started to type a sentence, deleted it then started again. 'I'm sure he'll appreciate your words.'

The troll replied, making her grin. She doubted that had been his intention. 'What do you think you are? Some sort of psychic?'

'As far from that as possible. Just someone in need of a bit of help.'

She ignored the negative comments from the troll, reading an anonymous reply. 'Do you need a hand?'

'We've got this. Jack and I.' She smiled. Somehow it made her feel a little less crazy knowing she wasn't the only one who Jack had helped.

'Be careful. His suggestions are a lot more sensible than you'll probably wish.'

Marti chuckled. Maybe Jack's suggestions were sensible, but she couldn't let Gordon sell the bike.

Chapter Ten

Marti

Before Marti could type in a comment, a sound had her turning towards her window. Her mouth dropped open when she saw Gordon climbing in. Closing the blog post, she rose from the desk to face him. "What are you doing in here?" Her room felt overly small and the bedroom door too far from her. Which was crazy. This was her uncle. Surely he wouldn't hurt her.

"You are going to get the bike for me right now."

She stared at him. Was he serious? "I'll scream." Sally would be in here in seconds.

"Do you really want to bring Sally into this? For now, Warren is willing to leave her out of it. That can easily change."

"So? Mum will call the cops."

Gordon smirked. "Think anyone will believe you? They know how badly you want the bike and that you're willing to do anything to keep it."

She hesitated.

"You know I'm right." He took a step towards her.

Dread pooled in the pit of her stomach and she backed away. Again she tried to remind herself that this was her uncle. She shouldn't be afraid of him. Not that she'd ever liked him, but he was family. Yet she took another step away from him. "She might not believe me about the bike, but she's going to have a lot of questions about why you're in my room at this hour."

"I can be out that window before she's in here." Gordon nodded towards the window he'd climbed through.

She started to tell him to get out of her room, deciding there was something she needed to know first. "What did you do with the will?"

"You're the only one who assumes there is one. The old man was pretty slack when it came to anything but that bike."

She hesitated, hoping he couldn't tell she was about to lie. "He showed it to me. The will. I'm not assuming anything. I know it exists." She watched the emotions race across his face.

Shock and worry were rapidly followed by another smirk. "Once again, your word against mine. We all know how badly you want the bike. You're wasting your time. You're not going to find the will anywhere in the old man's house." Gordon laughed softly. "No matter how much you search."

Anger rushed through her and her hands tightened into fists. She forced herself to remain where she stood. "Where is it? Where's the will?"

"Where's the bike? I can't stall them any longer. I'll be sending them in your direction. I'm not about to gain a broken finger for every day I'm late paying them their money."

Footsteps sounded along the hallway and she glanced over her shoulder towards the closed door. Facing Gordon again, she caught a glimpse of him as he disappeared through the window and into the night. What was he planning to do now?

"Marti?" Sally knocked on the bedroom door. "I'm heading to bed. It's time for you to go to bed too."

She opened the door to stare at Sally who had dark shadows under her eyes. For a moment she felt bad about all the dramas she was causing. But only for a moment. "Okay." Would Gordon really tell Warren he could hurt Sally? Surely it was an empty threat.

"And you will return the bike to Gordon

tomorrow. I don't want to have to bring your father in on this. The less I have to do with Hector, the better."

She badly wanted to argue. "Okay." She doubted Sally would be impressed if she told her she was working on a different plan. One that involved figuring out where Gordon had hidden the will. And he must have hidden it otherwise he would have worded his reply differently. He would have said she'd never be able to find it, not that she wouldn't find it in her grandad's house.

Sally frowned. "What are you up to?"

She hesitated. No, Gordon was right. It was her word against his. "Nothing."

"Then why no arguments?"

Marti sighed, trying to think of a plausible reason for her sudden compliance. She doubted Sally would believe she was worried about being grounded. That had never stopped her before. "I was going to ring Dad and ask him to take me to Grandad's house so I can look for the will. Obviously they aren't capable of finding it."

Sally started to shake her head. "Maybe that'd be best. Seeing for yourself that there isn't one. Do you want me to ring him?"

That was the last thing she needed. Especially since

she had no plans to involve Hector. "I can do it." Worried she'd answered too quickly, she added, "You'll get in an argument with him and he'll say no."

"All right. After you've looked, we're not to hear another word about the matter. You'll hand over the bike and stop causing problems. Agreed?"

"Unless I find the will. Then you have to help me keep the bike."

Sally didn't answer immediately. "All right. But you won't find one. Hector said he's searched the house and there's none."

She didn't point out that the spare room had barely been touched. She wasn't meant to have visited. "I guess we'll see."

Sally nodded once. "Goodnight. And get ready for bed."

"Okay." She remained in the doorway, watching Sally make her way to her own room, turning off the hallway light on the way past the switch. Leaving her door open, Marti turned off her bedroom light and locked the window, grabbing her backpack and heading for the back door where she'd left her sneakers. She had to get out of here before Gordon returned. Or worse. Warren. Surely he hadn't been serious when he'd said Warren would break fingers.

An image of Warren came to mind. A shudder ran through her. Maybe he had been serious.

She slipped outside, locking the door behind her and running to the back fence to clamber over it. She was halfway down the street when she came up with a plan. To search Gordon's house. He wasn't the brightest of people. Even Hector often said that.

Wishing she had a license, and a car, she jogged towards Gordon's place. It was ten minutes away and looked as bad as she remembered. The old Queenslander had the verandah across the front enclosed with fibro. One of the panels had a hole punched in it. She hurried around to the back of the house. At the front, it was three steps up from the ground. At the back, it was only a single one. Using the flashlight app on her phone she found the door was locked, the louvres on either side of it closed. After examining the door and surroundings, she found she could wriggle one of the louvres out of the frame by bending the metal.

Chapter Eleven

Marti

Leaning the louvre against the back wall, Marti put her hand inside to unlock the door, swinging it open. She stepped inside the kitchen. The smell of dirty dishes and an overflowing rubbish bin were overpowering. Not wanting to search the kitchen, she headed to the front of the house, doing a quick search in the room at the front. When she found nothing, she entered another room, sighing at the daunting task ahead of her. The place was a mess and filled with junk that probably should have been thrown out years ago.

The sound of a car door slamming shut had her turning off her flashlight app and holding her breath as she listened carefully. It was followed by the sound of a second car door. They seemed too close. She crept towards the front of the house, wincing when one of the floorboards creaked.

"I've got something to get rid of. You can wait in the car."

Shock arrowed through her at hearing Gordon's voice.

"You don't go anywhere without me," Warren warned.

"It won't take me long. A couple of minutes."

"You kept the will. How stupid are you?"

"No. Of course I didn't. I've got to get something from my bedroom."

"I thought you said you have to get rid of something."

"Yeah. From my bedroom."

"Then I'll go with you."

Marti hurried through the house, the arguing fading into the background. She'd been to Gordon's house only a couple of times. Each time with her grandad. So she knew the layout, just hadn't been in each room.

Reaching the bedroom, which was the room before the kitchen, she closed and locked the door, turning the flashlight app on and directing the light around the room. She screwed up her face at the piles of dirty clothes tossed in corners. There wasn't much in the room, which should make it easier to search.

By the time she heard footsteps coming down the hallway, she'd searched both bedside drawers, the nearly empty wardrobe in the corner and a large set of drawers at the foot of the bed. There was nowhere else to search and Gordon was coming closer, having turned on the hallway light, his complaints preceding him.

She glanced around the room. Had he been lying to Warren? The door handle rattled, the door shaking. It was too late. She had to leave. Disappointment crashed in on her. She'd lost. Gordon would sleep peacefully in his bed that night while she tossed and turned in hers thinking about how close she'd been.

"Open the door and get what you want. The boss wants to talk to you," Warren said.

"The door's stuck. I hate these old houses. If the rent wasn't such a good price…" His voice trailed off as the door rattled again.

She crept across the room to the window, needing to escape. Bed! She froze. It was the only place she hadn't checked. Scurrying to the bed, she lifted up the edge of the mattress, spotting several pieces of paper under it. She grabbed all of them, shoving them into her backpack as she lowered the mattress.

"Stand back. I'll get it open," Warren said.

Marti didn't worry about being quiet. Running for the window, she swept the curtain aside, pushing the window up so she could jump out. Behind her, Gordon yelled at Warren to hurry, the crack of timber as the door was flung open drowning his words. Marti landed on the ground, bending her knees to absorb the impact.

"Marti!" Gordon hung out the window. "You're going to regret this."

She ran, heading towards her school. They had a car and she was only on foot. She wasn't going to make it before they found her. Scanning the area, she looked for somewhere to hide. Turning a corner, she remembered a park at the end of the block. It was well treed with a playground in the middle. Surely there'd be somewhere she could hide in there. Behind her she heard a car starting. The neighbourhood was quiet, not even a dog barking. It had to be Gordon. She put on a burst of speed, pushing herself to reach the park, forcing herself not to glance over her shoulder. That would slow her down.

Reaching the park, she headed for a stand of trees, trying to slow her breathing. Glancing over her shoulder, she spotted them pull up at the front of the park, the headlights cutting a large path through the darkness. She headed further to her right and away from the light.

"Get back here," Gordon called out. A few seconds later, he bellowed, "Don't tell me what to do."

The stand of trees wasn't as thick as she'd remembered. They'd easily spot her. She headed further into the park, reaching someone's fence. A glance over her shoulder had her jumping the fence all the while hoping there were no vicious dogs in the yard. Her luck held and she ended up at the front of the house without disturbing anyone or anything. Not waiting around to see if they followed, she ran down the street, ignoring the ache in her legs.

Arriving at the school without seeing Gordon or Warren again, she headed for the groundsman's shed, using her flashlight app to find the way. She frowned as she noticed how low the charge was. A good thing there was a lantern in the shed. Jack stepped through the door and it swung open.

She grinned at him, heart still racing, relief rushing in on her at reaching safety. "I've got some messages for you." Passing along the messages seemed better than focusing on her problems.

"Messages?"

"Yeah." She headed for the space behind the wardrobe, closing the door of the shed first. "From people you've helped." She turned on the lantern and turned off the flashlight app.

"Marti-"

She interrupted him. "I'll show you." She brought up the comments of the blog post. He didn't deserve to wait after all the help he'd given her. She'd see what she'd taken from Gordon once she'd passed along the messages. A break from focusing on her problems would also be good.

He remained silent as he stared at the screen of her phone. "Can you tell them thank you? Tell them I'm glad they survived. And that I did very little compared to what each of them did."

She nodded, typing up his answer and ignoring the comments from the troll who at one stage asked if they were the Jack Richards' fan club. She grinned at the reply that said 'yes'. She lowered her phone. "Done."

"Thank you." He was sitting beside her, his arm resting on his drawn up leg. "Why are you here? I doubt you normally wander the streets this late at night."

She tucked her phone away. "I'm about to find out if Gordon was hiding Grandad's will." She took the papers out of her backpack, looking at the piece on top. She frowned, not making any sense of it. She checked the next one. They were mainly numbers along with strange word combinations.

"Racehorses?" Jack asked.

"What?"

He nodded towards the paper she held. "Are they racehorses?"

"I don't know." She took out her phone again and typed them in. "Greyhounds." She compared some of the details. "Either he's keeping notes on the winners he bets on or there's something else going on."

"Race fixing?" Jack asked.

She shrugged. What she knew about racing, greyhounds or horses, could be summed up in a single word. Nothing. She flicked through the pieces of paper, stopping at one that made her heart race. "Last will and testament." Her voice broke and she couldn't continue to read it out. The words danced in front of her and she brushed the tears away. It didn't help. More replaced them.

"It's yours. The bike is yours."

She tried to bring the will into focus, again wiping at tears. "He did leave it to me?"

"The house and contents are for his sons, the bike

for you because it wouldn't have been restored without your help and encouragement."

Chapter Twelve

Marti

A sound escaped Marti. Half laugh, half sob. "It's mine." The words finally came into focus. "They can't take it from me." Laughter bubbled up. "The bike is mine." She'd been right. They'd told her he hadn't left a will, yet he'd told her enough times that he had. She folded the will after taking note of the names of the witnesses at the bottom. She had no idea who they were. He'd had Justices Of The Peace witness his signature. "I need to ring Mum." She returned the paper to her backpack before taking her phone out. "She promised to-" She broke off when she saw the battery icon was flashing. "I need to go home." Rising to her feet, she captured Jack's hand. "Thank you."

"It's not over."

"But I found the will." She smiled. "I'll be back tomorrow to collect the bike. Will you look after it until then?"

His hand tightened on hers. "It's not over."

"Of course it is."

"Until I vanish and you can no longer see or hear me, it's not over."

"But–"

"You're still in danger."

She shook her head, drawing her hand from his grip. "I can't be. I found the will and Mum will help me fight for the bike. Everything is good."

Jack glanced at the phone. "Can you send someone a picture of the will?"

"I don't know." She took the will out again and unfolded it, placing it on the floor near the lantern. She took a picture, not daring to use the flash in case it used up the last of the phone's charge. Going to her list of contacts, she clicked on her mum's name and attached the image. She sent the image and waited to find out if it had gone through. Before she learned the answer, the phone went dead. "No." She pushed in the power button. Nothing happened.

"Did it go through?"

She shrugged. "I don't know." She glanced at the gap between the wardrobe and the wall. "I have to go home." Taking a step towards the gap, she turned back, worry from his earlier words bothering her. "How much danger?" When he frowned, she asked again, "How much danger am I in?"

Jack shrugged. "It's impossible to know."

She examined his face, trying to judge if he was telling the truth. She was beginning to think she wasn't very good at telling when people were lying. Especially after falling for Gordon's lies. "Guess."

"All the others have been in life threatening situations."

"Oh." She tried to swallow past the obstruction that seemed to have formed in her throat. "I could die?"

"I'm not about to let that happen."

"I can't spend the rest of my life hiding in here."

Jack grinned. "The groundsmen would have something to say about that when they turned up Monday or Tuesday."

She tried to think what the time had been when the phone went dead. It was after midnight, but other than that, she had no idea. "It's only Saturday. I can't stay here that long." She frowned as she tried to think of any phone boxes that were between her and home. If any still existed, she couldn't picture them. "Can I leave my backpack here?" Surely it'd be safer leaving it behind rather than taking it with her.

Jack nodded. "I'll look after your bag until you return for it. But I think you should stay here. At least until daylight."

That was ages away. "Thank you, but I'm going home." She used the lantern to find her way to the door, smiling at the bike when she walked past it. No one could take it from her. She glanced upwards. Could her grandad see what she'd accomplished? Was he happy the bike would be taken care of?

Turning off the lantern, she placed it on the floor beside the door before heading outside. There was barely enough light for her to stumble through the trees to the fence and clamber over it. She checked over her shoulder to find Jack watched her. He was wrong. Everything would be good now. All she had to do was go home and let everyone know she'd found the will. And she'd never have to worry about anyone taking the bike from her ever again.

She sighed. A pity she couldn't afford to catch a taxi. Not that she could call one even if she had the money to take one home. She was getting sick of all the walking she'd done lately. And running. Her body ached. Although a big part of it was probably from pushing the bike so far.

As she neared home, she headed down the street that was behind her house. About to enter the neighbour's yard, movement caught her attention. Warren burst out of the shadows, grabbing hold of her before she could get far. She struggled to escape, freezing when he pulled out a gun. Her gaze remained focused on the object, Jack's warning ringing in her mind. Why hadn't she listened? She could have at least waited until morning.

"I'm going to put the gun away and you're going to walk quietly beside me. Understand?"

She nodded, her gaze following the gun as he tucked it into a shoulder holster that was hidden by a light jacket he hadn't been wearing earlier.

"We'll walk to the end of the street and I'll call Gordon to pick us up."

Again she nodded. She felt tears burn her eyes, but she didn't let them fall. She'd been so close.

"Start moving." He took out a phone, his gaze never leaving her.

She kept glancing at him as he walked beside her, giving Gordon clipped orders before putting the phone away. They reached the corner before Gordon, standing there silently as they waited for him to arrive. She wanted to step away from Warren who stood far too close, but the image of the gun was burned into her mind and she didn't dare move away from him.

It was almost a relief when Gordon arrived and she was able to clamber into the back of the sedan. The relief was short lived. Warren joined her in the back. She eyed the door, discarding the idea of jumping out the moment the car moved off. She couldn't move faster than a bullet.

"Where to?" Gordon glanced over his shoulder.

"Where is the bike?" Warren demanded.

It was hers. She had proof. Her gaze was drawn to where the gun was hidden by Warren's jacket. But that didn't matter. It wouldn't protect her from a bullet. "School."

"Which school?" Warren asked.

"Mine. I hid it on the school grounds."

"No one better have stolen it," Gordon warned. "And where is what you stole from me?"

"You mean the will." She glared at the back of his head.

Gordon glanced over his shoulder. "Like anyone is going to believe you. Not after the stunts you've pulled in trying to keep my bike."

"It isn't yours. Grandad left it to me."

"Is she telling the truth?" Warren demanded.

"It won't matter. Not without a will to prove it. And everyone knows she's desperate to try any trick to keep it," Gordon said.

Chapter Thirteen

Marti

Marti opened her mouth to say she'd sent a picture of the will to Sally. She closed her mouth instead. What would they do if she told them that? Kill her? Kill Sally? Again her gaze was drawn to Warren's jacket. How badly did he want the bike? Or was it only the money Gordon owed that was important. And they didn't care how they got the money. Warren and his mysterious boss.

Gordon chuckled. "Guess that shut you up. No smart comments to make? No threats?"

She pressed her lips tightly together, not wanting to give him the satisfaction of saying anything.

"Where at the school?" Warren asked.

"I'll show you when we get there." Would he have a reason to keep her alive if she told him? Once she would have thought Gordon would never hurt her. As inconsiderate and rude as he was he'd never go far enough to harm a family member. Or let someone else harm them. Now she was no longer sure what he was capable of.

"Where do I park?" Gordon demanded. "And don't even think of mentioning out the front. That entrance is lit up like a Christmas tree."

She automatically started to argue that a couple of lights weren't enough to light up an area that much. Again she closed her mouth with a glance at Warren.

"Well?" Gordon glanced over his shoulder. "Where do I park?"

She mentally pictured the school grounds, trying to think of the best location. One that wasn't too close to the groundsman's shed. Somewhere that would give her a chance to escape. "Take the next street after the main entrance. It'll bring us around to the back entrance. It's less lit up."

"Is that where you left the bike?" Gordon asked.

"You didn't want to park near the main entrance."

"You better not be leading us on a wild goose chase," Gordon warned.

She glanced at Warren who remained silent beside her. "The bike is here. My bike is here." She stressed the word 'my'.

Gordon chuckled. "Not as far as everyone else is concerned."

Again she pressed her lips together, not daring to speak the words that came to mind. Not with Warren sitting beside her. She doubted it'd take long for him to draw his gun.

Gordon pulled up and they got out of the vehicle. He rested a hand heavily on her shoulder. She wanted to pull away. Steeling herself she remained at his side.

Warren took out his phone. "Keep walking, but don't go too far ahead. I've got to check in with the boss."

Gordon entered the back entrance of the school, his grip tight on her shoulder, using his phone to light the way. "Don't think about running." He jerked his head in Warren's direction. "He won't hesitate to shoot."

Jack strode towards her. "Do you want me to cause a distraction?"

She looked from Jack to Gordon.

Jack chuckled. "Only you can see me." He stopped in front of Gordon, letting him walk straight through him.

She winced, glancing over her shoulder at Jack. "Not yet."

Gordon's grip tightened. "You're not running. Not now and not later. Do you want to die?"

"I can't do much more than make classroom doors fly open." Jack walked beside her. "Tell me when you want me to do that."

She nodded, about to answer Jack, when Gordon spoke.

"Why would you want to die?" He shook her shoulder.

"I don't want to die."

"Then why nod?"

She glanced at Jack, having no idea what to say.

Warren joined them. "Where is the bike? I want this over and done with. I have another job to deal with before daybreak."

They walked past a block of classrooms and Marti glanced at them. "Jack." She spoke his name softly, hoping it was loud enough he could hear.

"Speak up," Warren said.

"You want a distraction now?" Jack asked.

"Yes." Again she spoke softly.

Warren moved Gordon out of the way so he could walk beside her. "Don't mumble. Where is the bike?"

She glanced at Jack, who strode towards the door of the nearest classroom. "I'll show you."

A classroom door slammed open, catching Warren

and Gordon's attention. When they both stopped and looked in that direction, Gordon shining the light from his phone that way, Marti bolted.

"Stop," Warren called out.

Jack caught up with her, grabbing her hand and tugging her amongst the buildings. The sound of gunfire had her stumbling.

"Put that away. Do you want someone to call the cops," Gordon called after Warren.

Marti kept running, the sound of pursuit behind her. Ahead the grounds were in darkness and she struggled to see where she was going. She tried to head in a different direction. One with more light.

Jack grasped her hand tightly. "This way. Put some distance between you and them and you'll be able to hide."

She wanted to tell him she couldn't run much further. Even with his help, tugging her out of the path of obstacles, it was becoming harder to maintain her pace without tripping. But that might catch Warren's attention. Not that she had the breath for speaking. She breathed harshly, the pound of her heart echoing the sound of the footsteps that followed.

"This way. And when I tell you, jump over

something that is at calf height. Take a larger jump than you think necessary," Jack said.

She couldn't protest without letting Warren know about the obstacle ahead. But she wanted to tell him he was crazy if he thought she could manage to jump over something in the dark.

"Now."

She leapt over something she couldn't see, continuing to run, amazed she hadn't ended up sprawled across the ground face first. Behind her Warren crashed into something, calling out threats and demanding Gordon hurry up and help. She smiled. Somehow, she'd made it. She wasn't about to let either of them win. The bike was hers.

"Over here." Jack tugged her in the direction he wanted her to go.

Plants brushed against her face and she couldn't help thinking about the cobwebs she'd run into in the garden shed. It'd be worse running into cobwebs if she couldn't see them at all. She tried not to think of spiders, but her mind was filled with eight legged, hairy creatures that grew larger by the second.

"Walk. There's a wall coming up. Hide behind this shrub that's against the wall. When you reach the wall, crouch."

She opened her mouth to tell him she couldn't see

the shrub. Then she felt it brush against her arm. Or at least she assumed it was the shrub. Stretching out a hand, she found the wall. Crouching caused her calves to ache so she sat on the damp ground, dew seeping into her jeans. She shivered. About to ask Jack where Warren was, she heard Gordon speak.

"How could you have let her get away?"

"She's your niece," Warren argued.

"I wasn't the one standing beside her. You pushed me out of the way."

She caught a flash of light from Gordon's phone, leaning forward as she tried to catch the rest of their conversation.

"Stop shining that around everywhere. Are you trying to blind me?" Warren demanded. "And be quiet. How are we meant to hear her if you won't stop talking?"

"It wouldn't be a problem if you hadn't let her go," Gordon said. "Don't point that at me."

"Then be quiet."

Marti pressed herself against the wall at the menace she heard in Warren's voice, covering her mouth with her hand. She dreaded to think what he'd do if he caught her.

"They're moving further away. Give them a few

minutes before you find somewhere better to hide," Jack said.

Chapter Fourteen

Marti

Marti half lowered her hand, keeping her voice low. "I don't want to find somewhere else to hide. I want to go home."

"I'll see where they are and let you know if it's safe to leave."

"Okay." She remained pressed against the wall, chilled by the damp ground and the wall at her back. She had no idea how long she sat there, but it felt like ages.

"If you head straight to the main entrance, you'll be safe."

She pressed a hand against her racing heart. "Don't do that to me."

"Do what?" Jack asked.

She struggled to her feet, her legs uncooperative

after how long she'd been sitting on the cold, damp ground. "Scare me like that. Can't you make a noise or something? It's not like I can see in the dark."

"I'm a ghost, Marti," he said dryly.

"I know that. I don't have any idea what that has to do with what I said." She took a cautious step forward, running into the shrub.

"I can't interact with the world around me." Jack took her hand and drew her around the shrub. "Other than whoever I'm helping. So I don't make a sound when walking."

She clung to his hand, stumbling as she tried to see her surroundings. All she could see were shadows and glimpses of light in the distance. "Where are they?"

"They split up to cover more ground. Keep moving and we'll be out of here before they can get around to checking the main entrance."

She thought of her backpack, hidden in the groundsman's shed. She'd come back for it later. It would be crazy to go after it now. She came to an abrupt stop. "What if they find my bike?" She didn't want to lose it after all she'd gone through.

"I locked the door. It's safe. Safer than you are."

"Thank you." Ahead she saw the lights at the main entrance. "And thank you for helping me escape."

"It's not over yet," Jack warned.

She smiled. "I'm not about to come back here on my own." Did he think she was stupid? She didn't want to die.

"If you can see me, it's not over," Jack reminded her.

"I know." She kept walking towards the exit, thinking of all the students who wished they could say one more thing to Jack. "So I'll thank you now since I'm sure you'll disappear once I leave the school grounds."

"It doesn't work like that."

"Well, maybe I'll have to be down the road a bit. But when I come back, with the police, you'll probably be gone."

"I hope so." Jack stopped by the entrance. "This is as far as I can go."

She faced him. "Goodbye, Jack."

"Run as fast as you can and don't stop for any reason."

"Okay." Her gaze travelled over him one more time before she turned and started jogging along the footpath. Reaching the corner, she slowed when she saw a car pull up in the next street. She glanced over her shoulder. Should she cross the road? Or take a circuitous route home?

A man got out of the car and walked around to the

passenger side, opening the door to let out a dog. He held the lead while the dog sniffed the ground.

Relief washed over her. The dog had obviously needed to get out of the car. She slowly walked towards the man who took out a phone and stared at the screen while he waited for the dog to finish. Her gaze remained on the phone. She didn't need to go home and risk being caught along the way. She could ask for help. It wasn't like she had to get close to him to have him call the police.

He glanced up as she drew near, returning his attention to the phone.

"Hello."

Another glance and a nod before he looked at the screen of his phone again.

"Can you help me? Can you call the police?"

The man lowered his phone, giving her his full attention. "Why do you need the police called?"

She hadn't expected that. Staying well back out of his reach, she gathered her thoughts. "I was attacked by two men and barely managed to escape." She didn't want to waste time giving a full explanation.

"Well now, that is unfortunate."

For a moment she couldn't figure out what to say. Did he think she was joking? "Ahh… yes."

"One of those men wouldn't happen to be called Warren."

Her stomach sank like she was on the downward drop of a roller coaster. But not in a good way. Questions rushed through her mind as she took a step back, not voicing a single one. Each question would have confirmed that one of the men was called Warren. "You're not going to call the police?" She tried to think of a way to stall him as she backed away, wishing the streetlight on the other side of the street cast enough light for her to see his expression more clearly.

"Bingo." He took a step towards her.

"Sorry about this, Boss."

Marti spun to see Warren walking towards her. She backed away towards the street, turning so she could see both of them. A glance around showed Gordon wasn't visible.

"You might want to stay still. Warren has a habit of ruining kneecaps when people try to run."

She glanced at the man Warren called boss, not about to ask him for a name. She remained still, her gaze returning to Warren who was close enough he could touch her. Or hit her. She steeled herself.

Warren grabbed her shoulder, dragging her close,

his voice low. "How did you make the door slam open like that? Who else is here with you?"

"I didn't. And I don't know."

"You're saying it was a coincidence."

"It distracted you. So I ran."

"What's going on, Warren?"

Warren kept his gaze on her a moment longer before he looked at his boss. "Making sure she isn't leading us into some sort of trap."

"Arlo." Gordon joined them on the footpath, looking between the two men. "What are you doing here?"

"The better question would be, why should I need to be here?" Arlo asked.

"Ah… well… uhm." Gordon cleared his throat. "I blame my sister-in-law. Lack of discipline. If she hadn't let Marti get away with so much…" His voice trailed off and he took a step back from Arlo.

"Deal with it before I lose patience. You really don't want to find out what happens when I lose my patience," Arlo said.

Marti wanted to back away like her uncle did, but Warren continued to grip her shoulder tightly. She wasn't going anywhere.

"Are you planning to stand here till daylight?" Arlo demanded.

"Ahh… no." Gordon grabbed hold of Marti's arm, just above her elbow. "Where is the bike?" He dragged her out of Warren's grip, the light from his phone shining on the ground.

Chapter Fifteen

Marti

Marti gestured towards the exit, trying not to look at the treed area that hid the groundsman's shed.

"Start moving." Gordon kept hold of her arm.

She stumbled as he dragged her towards the entrance. Jack was waiting for her and she half expected him to tell her he'd told her so.

"Do you want me to unlock the door of the groundsman's shed?" Jack walked on the other side of Gordon, the men remaining close to her so he wasn't able to walk at her side. "The bike isn't worth your life."

She shook her head, wishing she could tell him it might buy her some time. But she couldn't. Not without giving away her plan. If it could be considered a plan.

"You better not be sending us on a wild goose chase," Gordon said.

"No." She glanced at Jack, relieved he remained with her.

"What are you looking at?" Gordon also looked to the side.

"I thought I saw movement." She glanced at Jack again. "Must have been a moth or something drawn by your light."

Jack chuckled. "Nice save."

She barely managed not to smile. That would have had Gordon asking more questions. Probably make Warren suspicious too. She stopped in front of the door to the groundsman's shed. "It's in here."

Warren tried the handle. "It's locked."

She nodded. "Of course it is. I put the bike in there this morning when it was unlocked."

"How do you know one of the groundsmen didn't steal it?" Gordon demanded. "How stupid are you leaving a bike like that lying around?"

She winced when his grip tightened painfully. "I didn't leave it lying around. I hid it."

"Step back and I'll get it open," Warren said.

"All the buildings have alarms." She nearly fell when Gordon jerked her away from the door.

"What are you doing?" Jack demanded. "Are you

trying to get yourself killed? I'll open the door and they can have the bike."

She wanted to tell him no, but was only able to shake her head slightly. "If you break that door down, security will be here within minutes."

Warren chuckled. "You think we're stupid? Security doesn't respond that quickly. Now step back."

"What do you want me to do?" Jack asked.

She looked from Warren to Jack. "Open it then." She returned her attention to Warren. "Don't blame me if something goes wrong. It's a school. Students tend to cause trouble during the holidays so the security company is more prompt at responding to alarms during holidays. And on long weekends."

"That makes sense," Gordon said.

"Does that mean you want me to open it?" Jack asked.

She tried to think of a way to answer Jack. She stared directly at him. "When you open it, or should I say if you open it, that can only help me."

"You're going to have to be clearer than that," Jack said.

Warren dragged her out of Gordon's grip, his face close to hers. "You better not be lying to me."

Her mouth went dry and she shook her head, unable to speak.

"Marti, do you want me to open the door?"

She forced the word past her lips, hoping Jack knew she was answering him. "No."

"I hope you know what you're doing," Jack said.

She wasn't so sure she did. She was making it up as she went along.

Warren shoved her from him and she nearly fell. He turned to Gordon. "This is not our problem. You're the one who owes money."

She slowly backed away, ready to run the moment she had the chance.

"She took some of the notes," Gordon said.

Warren grabbed a fistful of Gordon's shirt and slammed him against the wall of the shed. "Say that again."

"The notes. The ones Arlo gave me."

Spinning, Marti ran, not waiting to find out what Warren planned to do next. She kept her hands outstretched, hoping to avoid running into something.

Jack grabbed hold of her hand, dragging her to the side. "This way." He tugged her to the side again. "Watch the tree."

"I can't see anything other than shadows." And the shadows she could see blended into each other.

"What were you trying to tell me about the door earlier?" Jack guided her through the trees.

A gunshot sounded behind her and she flinched. "I only wanted you to open the door if he tried to open it." She stumbled, kept upright by Jack's grip on her. "I was hoping he'd fall on the floor and I could make a run for it."

"I didn't get that message from your words." Jack chuckled. "It might have worked though."

"Where are we going?"

"How do you feel about hiding on a roof?"

"I'm not tall enough to manage that." They left the trees behind and she wanted to run back amongst them, feeling too exposed even though it was night.

"I'll help you. Now be quiet so they don't hear where you've gone."

She remained silent, her feet pounding on the ground and her heart beating in her ears the only sounds. Her lungs began to feel like they burned, as did her legs. She was fairly active, but all this running around was getting to be too much. About to ask how much further, Jack slowed, drawing her close to a building. "On-"

"Quiet. They aren't that far back." He helped her

onto the roof before joining her. "Lie flat. I'll see what they're doing."

She wanted to protest, not wanting to be left alone. He was gone before she had the chance. She lay flat on the roof of the athletics shed, the cold of the corrugated metal sheeting seeping into her body. Remaining pressed against the roof, she lifted her head several times to look around the area. Nothing. Or at least nothing she could see.

Again she lifted her head. She saw nothing and heard nothing. Should she try and escape? Try and head home. Eventually, day would arrive and there'd be no shadows to hide in. It wasn't like she could spend the rest of the weekend on the roof of the athletics shed.

Jack joined her on the roof. "You need to leave. Immediately. Need a hand down?"

Chapter Sixteen

Marti

"What's going on?" Marti came up in a crouch, scanning the area.

"Warren has gone to get Arlo's dog to find you."

"Oh." She looked over the edge of the roof. The distance seemed further from up here.

"Need a hand?" Jack asked again.

"Yeah."

He helped her down, joining her on the ground. "Avoid the entrance. Go straight home. Don't stop for anything."

She once more expected him to tell her he'd told her so. He didn't. She scanned the area. "I need my bike." It didn't matter that she had no license or helmet to wear. If the police pulled her over it'd actually be a good thing.

"Are you trying to get yourself killed?"

"No. That's why I need my bike. If they spot me, there's no way I can run. I'm exhausted." It was going to be hard enough wheeling the bike out of the groundsman's shed. She was going to feel every bit of its weight.

Jack faced her for a moment before turning away. "I'll meet you there. Let me check where they are."

He was gone before she could protest. How was she meant to find her way in the dark through the trees? Sighing, she hurried towards the groundsman's shed, unable to run. Her body was protesting moving as fast as she was. She was tired and wanted to sleep. It had been an extremely long day. Reaching the trees, she slowed, stretching her hands out as she tried to find her way without running into one of them. It didn't help as much as she'd hoped. Wincing, she rubbed her shoulder where she'd clipped a tree.

"Here." Jack spoke as he took her hand. "They're going to hear you from miles away with the amount of noise you're making."

"Unlike you, I can't see in the dark. Which you didn't give me a chance to say before you ran off."

"Can you walk faster? They'll find you before you can escape."

"I'm going as fast as I can." It was easier walking

through the dark holding onto his hand. She ran into fewer things.

"Here we are. Wait there while I unlock the door." Jack let go of her hand.

She wanted to protest, wrapping her arms around herself instead. The night, or early morning, was getting cooler. It didn't help that her clothes were damp from dew, both from sitting on the ground and lying on the roof. The click of the door unlocking had her lowering her arms.

Jack took her hand again. "It doesn't always unlock straight away."

"That's okay." She wouldn't have survived the night without his help. Gordon might think no one would believe her, but she had a bad feeling Arlo preferred to tie up loose ends. Permanently. With the help of Warren. She followed him inside, clinging to his hand, wishing she could see where she was going. It was even more impossible to see inside. There weren't even shadows of varying darkness. She stumbled. "I can't see anything at all."

"I'll guide you to–" He broke off. "Wait here."

Once more he was gone before she could protest. Frustration arrowed through her. When he returned she'd tell him exactly how little she appreciated that. When someone grabbed her hand, a scream almost escaped. A hand clamped over her mouth, preventing any sound from escaping.

"It's me. Close the door." Jack removed his hand from her mouth, drawing her back to the door. "Hurry. And stay quiet."

She carefully closed the door he'd placed her hand against, hearing the click of it locking. "What's going on?" Remembering the lantern she'd left by the door, she reached for it.

"No. Don't turn it on. They'll see it." Jack grabbed her hand, drawing her back from the door.

"What is going on?" She asked again.

"They're bringing the dog back here since it was the last location, they know for certain, that you were in." Jack drew her away from the door.

"I'm trapped. There's only one exit." Fear rushed through her and she tried to pull away from Jack.

He wrapped his arms around her, keeping her in place. "The door is locked. They won't think you're in here. It's not like you have a key."

She leaned heavily against him. He felt real. "How can you be a ghost?"

Jack laughed softly. "Haven't we already covered this? Although you did accept it a lot easier than the others have."

"It was a little hard not to when the wheel of my

bike was in your body." She drew back from him, his arms still around her. "They're not going to let me live, are they? Gordon is wrong. People will believe me when I tell them what happened."

"Shh. They're close."

She hadn't needed him to tell her. The dog, that regularly barked, sounded metres away. She closed her eyes tightly. She wanted to go home. But she didn't dare move. Not with them so close. She barely dared to breathe.

"Don't move. I'll go outside and see what they're doing." Jack let her go.

He was gone before she could protest. She should be getting used to that habit of his, but she wasn't. Outside Gordon's phone rang. He was at the side of the groundsman's shed. Far closer than she liked.

"Why are you ringing me at this hour of the morning?" There was a short pause before Gordon spoke again. "How would I know where your daughter is? What sort of a parent are you that you don't know?"

Marti frowned. Was that her mum?

"What do you mean she sent you a copy of the will?" Gordon demanded. "There is no will. It has to be a fake. I knew she was determined to have the bike, but I didn't think she'd go to those sorts of extremes."

It was her mum. Marti took a step towards the door. Before she could move, Jack's arms went around her.

He clamped a hand over her mouth. "You can't go out there. Warren and the dog are directly in front of the door. Don't even speak." He let go of her.

She mouthed the word 'please', gesturing towards the door. Didn't he understand? That was her mum on the phone. And she knew about the will. From the sounds of Gordon's side of the conversation, Sally didn't believe what he was saying.

Jack guided her away from the door, helping her avoid the many items in the groundsman's shed that she could trip over. "You can't go out there."

Once she was near the wardrobe she spoke, keeping her voice as low as possible. "You have to unlock the door."

"No."

"That's my mum on the phone. I need to let her know where I am."

"If you let her know, the rest will know."

"I can't stay in here. They'll eventually find me."

"You need to wait until they move away. Give it a minute and I'll go out there and see if I can distract the dog. Animals might not be able to see me, but they can often sense me and don't like it when I'm nearby. And especially don't like it when I walk through them."

"You can draw them away?" She tried to see in the darkness. It was impossible.

"Don't move. There are too many things you might run into and I can't promise both of them will follow the dog. Wait until I return for you."

"Okay." She nodded, wishing she had the lantern and dared turn it on. She glanced at the area behind the wardrobe that she couldn't see. "Can I have the lantern on if I hide behind the wardrobe?"

Jack didn't answer immediately. "All right. I'll help you collect it before I leave. But it might be best to shade most of its light with the cushion."

"I can do that." She would have agreed to almost anything rather than be left alone in the dark.

Chapter Seventeen

Marti

It took longer than Marti expected to return to the door where the lantern had been left. Outside the dog barked excitedly and Warren urged it to find her.

"Think she might've climbed up on the roof?" Gordon asked.

"I wouldn't have thought she was tall enough to get up there. You go up and check," Warren said.

"You've got to be joking," Gordon exclaimed. "Are you trying to get me killed?"

"Can't get money out of a dead man." Warren paused a moment. "Which is why I prefer to break fingers."

Marti drew in a sharp breath as she grabbed the lantern, hoping no one had heard her. The matter-of-fact way Warren had spoken sent a chill down her spine. He might be willing to keep Gordon alive because he owed money, but she didn't owe him anything.

"Are you all right?" Jack asked.

She nodded, immediately shaking her head only to nod again. She had no idea how she was. About the only condition she could comment on was the physical. She wasn't as cold while inside, but nor was she warm since her clothes were damp. Apart from that, she had no idea.

"Ready to return to the back corner of the shed?"

She nodded. Wishing she could speak. A scrape against the roof had her looking upwards. Was that Gordon? She allowed Jack to lead her through the room, cautiously stepping where he told her.

"Put more effort into it than that or you will break your neck," Warren said.

"I told you," Gordon snapped.

Marti grinned at the scrabbling sound on the roof. She hoped he did fall. Without breaking his neck though. Reaching the area behind the wardrobe, she turned on the lantern, shielding it with her body as she crouched and picked up the cushion. The dim glow the lantern cast, once shielded by the cushion, wasn't much. But it was better than remaining in the dark now Jack had left.

"Where are you going?" Gordon demanded.

Marti looked upwards. It had sounded like he was finally on the roof.

"Looks like the dog has picked up her trail," Warren said.

"Then why did you make me come up here?" Gordon demanded.

"Get down before she gets too far away," Warren ordered.

Marti looked towards the door at the sound of a thud. It had been too soft for it to have been Gordon.

"Now look what you made me do. If my phone is broken you owe me a new one."

"Get down here now, Gordon. Or I'm leaving you behind."

"I can't see what I'm doing. I dropped my phone. Shine your torch over here," Gordon said.

Marti grinned at the sound of her uncle muttering and moving around on the roof. She doubted he'd be complaining about Warren if he hadn't walked away a few metres. Even muttering under his breath. Her smile faded when she heard Warren's reply.

"I don't have time for this. Find your own way down or stay up there."

"Come back. Don't leave me up here," Gordon called out.

She waited for Warren to answer. There was none. He'd left Gordon behind? She looked upwards when there was more scrambling on the roof. How was she meant to escape with Gordon above her?

She took out her phone, once more trying to turn it on. It was impossible. There was absolutely no charge. The only way she was going to get help was to go out there and get it herself. And that meant making it past Gordon. Her gaze was once again drawn upwards as she put her phone away. How badly was he stuck? Would he find a way down if he was desperate enough? Like if she tried to ride out of here on her bike.

Jack walked through the wardrobe. "Looks like your uncle can't get down. You still want to ride out of here? It'll be daylight soon."

She stared at him. "Daylight?" Her heart skipped a beat when he nodded. "Are you sure Warren is far enough away?"

Jack nodded. "If you leave now."

It took her a few seconds to come to a decision. Nodding, she rose to her feet and collected her backpack, slipping her arms through the straps. "Let's do this." Before she changed her mind.

"Put the lantern out and I'll guide you to the bike."

Jack nodded towards the lantern mostly hidden by the cushion.

She didn't want to turn it off. Didn't want to be in the dark again. Taking a deep breath, she turned off the lantern. She released her breath in a rush, surprised it wasn't as dark as it had been earlier. Not that she could see anything. It just wasn't pitch black.

Jack guided her to the bike and placed her hand on the seat. She smiled. The familiarity of it was comforting. She ran her hand across the leather.

"Will you be able to start it in the dark?"

She smiled in Jack's direction, nodding. She knew every inch of this bike. Light wouldn't be necessary.

"The moment you start the bike, I'll make the door fly open. So be ready." Jack paused a moment. "Hopefully."

"Thank you, Jack." She said the words as quietly as possible, aware of Gordon above her.

"It's not over yet."

She smiled at the humour in his voice. "I know. But this time it will be. I'm not going to stop for anything."

"Good. Go home. Live."

She nodded as she ran her hands over the bike, pulling the fuel tap out, setting the ignition control lever and pressing the carburettor priming button several times. The actions were so familiar. She'd done them hundreds of times with her grandad. Had also ridden the bike from the garage he'd had built onto the side of his house and into the backyard where they'd always cleaned the bike. A few times he'd let her ride it around the backyard. A smile formed as she thought of her grandad. She might not need the bike to remember him, but there was no way she'd be able to forget him whenever she looked at it.

"Should I open the door now?" Jack asked.

She kicked up the centre stand, nodding her head as she kick started the bike. It caught instantly. The muted, rhythmic thump filled the shed. At the same time, the door flew open.

"Who's down there? Marti? Is that you?" Gordon called down.

She pushed the bike out of the groundsman's shed, swinging her leg over the seat. It was bright enough outside that she could see the shadowy figure of her uncle leaning over the edge of the roof. She couldn't resist smiling up at Gordon, then gave a nod to Jack before she took off, heading for the front entrance.

"Warren! She's here. Warren," Gordon called out.

She left him behind, riding through the grounds, slowing as she went out the main gate. She slowed further, coming to a stop when she saw a police car parked in front of Arlo's vehicle, the officer talking to him. Arlo shrugged and the officer nodded, Arlo starting to walk around the front of his car. Anger rushed through her. She wasn't about to let him get away with it. With any of it.

A glance over her shoulder showed Jack was behind her, striding towards the main gate. Facing forward, she raced towards the two cars, braking when the police officer faced her. She pressed the kill switch that was on the handlebar. "Don't let him get away." Dismounting, she kicked the stand down as Arlo ran to his car door.

The police officer caught him before he could make it, a second officer stepping out of the parked vehicle. "Are you Martine?"

She nodded.

The officer slowly shook his head. "What is it about this school that the students come here when they're in trouble?"

She glanced towards the main gate. Jack was nowhere in sight. Did that mean she was safe? Again she faced the officer, shrugging. She could have told him it wasn't something, it was someone. But that would have caused other problems and led to questions she couldn't answer.

"Your mother is waiting back at the station for you," the officer said.

The second one marched Arlo towards them. "He said you chased his dog away and he's been stuck here trying to call him back. That you asked him for the use of his phone and when he offered to ring your mum, you scared away his dog, demanding the phone."

"He tried to help my uncle steal my bike. And they're doing something with greyhounds. I have some papers I got from my uncle." She took them from her backpack, keeping the will. "Uncle Gordon and Warren are still in the school grounds. And Warren has a gun."

The moment she spoke the word 'gun', everything changed. Before she knew it, more officers arrived and she was being taken to the police station, one of them assuring her that the bike would be taken care of. She stared out the back window of the police car, looking from the bike to the school grounds. She hadn't seen Jack since she'd spoken to the police. Sadness washed over her. She'd miss him.

Chapter Eighteen

Jack

Jack strode inside the groundsman's shed, glad the school grounds were empty again. He'd been worried about the fuzz that had apprehended Gordon. He'd kept saying how odd it was that the kids attending this school came here when they were in trouble, instead of somewhere more sensible. One of them had mentioned that it would have been the last place he would have gone to, back when he was at school, so it was lucky his fellow officer had checked here on a hunch. Jack had winced when the first officer had said that after the last two times he'd been called out to the school, it was the first place he'd thought of when he'd learned what school Marti attended.

He sighed. He really needed to have a talk to that blasted bird. What happened if people knew of his existence? People other than the ones he was helping. He stared down at the cushion that was resting against the lantern. A pity he couldn't tidy up in here. He tried, forcing his hand through the cushion several times. It didn't move.

A sound outside had him walking through the wall. He stopped, surprised to see Marti heading to the front of the groundsman's shed, wearing her usual backpack. It took a few seconds to recover and hurry after her. He smiled when she knocked on the door as if expecting someone to answer it.

"Jack? Are you home?" She frowned. "In there. I mean, it could be your home. Sort of."

He chuckled, striding through the door so it unlocked. He hadn't expected her to turn up for days. Maybe not even until school went back in.

"Thanks, Jack." She opened the door, taking out her phone and using the flashlight app to find her way to the area behind the wardrobe. "Sorry I left the place in a mess." She turned on the lantern and turned off her app, putting the cushion in the corner. "I've got something for you. Well, several things actually." She took off her backpack and rummaged inside it, taking out two phone chargers. "In case someone else needs their phone charged." She put them near the cushion.

Jack chuckled. "They might come in handy."

"And this is for you." She took out a photo and used blu tack to stick it to the wall next to the photo of Rose.

Jack came closer, his smile fading as he stared at the image of the bike. The 1953 Royal Enfield Bullet. It was Marti's bike, but so similar to the one he'd owned there were barely any differences. "Marti-" He broke off, clearing his throat even though she wouldn't have heard his voice break. "Thank you, Marti."

She glanced around the area. "Mum didn't want me to go anywhere. She tried to tell me I was grounded for a year. I pointed out the bike had been gone before she got home so I couldn't be. I talked her down to no parties or the movies for a month."

Jack chuckled. It didn't surprise him. She was persistent. Her mum probably hadn't stood a chance.

"I tried to stay home. Even hopped online and checked the blog post. There was another reply. They said 'I wish I could do even a fraction for you of what you did for me.' I had to tell them I could no longer talk to you. Which I guess isn't exactly true. I mean, I can talk to you, I just can't hear any answers you might give."

"I wish you could hear me."

"I thought about the message I'd want you to have.

You're right. Some people are impossible to forget. Even without reminders, I'll never forget you. I left it as a comment. Maybe the next person you help can give me your reply."

"I'll never forget you either. None of you," Jack said.

"The troll had to comment about how insane we all are. They were going on that we might as well create a Jack Richards fan club page. Someone said we should. That they had the perfect title. 'Jack Richards. Sinner or saint?' I don't think the troll was impressed."

Jack chuckled, slowly shaking his head at her comment. "A fan club." Again he shook his head.

Marti glanced towards the gap. "I should probably go home." She sighed. "I had to escape for a while. Mum has been hovering over me since I arrived at the station this morning. I told her I had to get out and take a walk or I'd go crazy from all the attention. It took a bit to convince her. I wanted to let you know I was okay." She grinned. "And my bike is okay too."

"I knew you'd be okay. The moment you could no longer see me I knew you were safe," Jack said.

"You should have seen the cop that brought my bike home. He looked too young to be a police officer. Anyway, he asked if I was keeping it or was interested in selling. There's no way I'm selling my bike. Even if it hadn't taken a lot of effort to prove it was mine."

Jack glanced at the photo she'd put on the wall. "I don't blame you." He couldn't help wondering what had happened to his bike when he'd died. His father had probably got rid of it. He'd never liked it.

Marti crouched by the lantern, her hand resting on it. She didn't turn it off, looking around the area once more. "You should have seen my dad. He came storming into the police station demanding to know where Uncle Gordon was. He looked murderous. They wouldn't let him see his brother. Not that I blame them. He kept asking me if I was okay and if Uncle Gordon had hurt me. Apparently, he fell off the roof. Didn't break anything." She grinned. "Not even his neck."

Jack nodded. "It was a satisfying sight."

"No one will tell me what happened to Warren. Other than he was caught. It would have been nice if he'd fallen off a building too."

Jack grinned. "Worse. He got tangled up in the dog's lead when he tried to escape. He came back when Gordon called him, then tried to bolt when he saw the fuzz. By the time he thought to let go of the lead, it was too late." It hadn't taken much effort to send the dog in circles after his earlier attempts at convincing the dog to lead Warren away from the groundsman's shed.

She shrugged. "I suppose it isn't important. They did tell me the three of them were involved in race fixing." She took out her phone and turned on the flashlight app before she turned off the lantern. She rose to her feet. "One of the cops kept asking me why students from my school run here when they're in danger. He wanted to know what is it about this place that makes us think it's a safe haven. I obviously couldn't tell him. All I could say is that it's a good school. One where we're made to feel safe." She smiled wryly. "That led to questions about bullying. It was a bit hard to know what to say since I'd just finished saying it was a safe school. Luckily Mum demanded to know why they were bothering me with useless questions."

Jack followed Marti outside where she once again paused, looking at the door she closed.

"Will you mind if I visit sometimes? Let you know how life is going. Tell you about my bike." She grinned. "It'd save me having to annoy my parents with my monologues about it."

Jack nodded. "I'd appreciate it."

"Maybe next time a student needs help you can ask them to leave me a message in the comments of the blog post. Let me know if it's okay." She stood there a moment longer before she strode towards the front entrance, looking over her shoulder once.

Jack watched her go, smiling. He was looking forward to her monologues. And looking forward to the next student he could help. A chuckle escaped as he slowly shook his head. A fan club. That was the last thing he'd expected her to mention. And the last thing he could imagine having. He strode inside, locking the door on the first attempt. He already knew the answer to the question. He was no saint.

Free Ebook

Subscribe to Avril's newsletter and receive a free ebook. This ebook is exclusive to those on her mailing list. To find out more about this offer visit:

www.avrilsabine.com/free-ebook

*

We value your privacy and will not sell, rent, exchange or loan your email address to third parties. Your information is confidential and you are under no obligation to remain on the mailing list and can unsubscribe at any time.

Acknowledgements

Like always, many thanks to the usual crew. I appreciate your help.

To The Reader

If you enjoyed this book, why not consider leaving a review to help other readers discover it too? Reader engagement is one of the few ways that lets an author know readers want more books in a particular series or genre. So leave a review and tell friends, not only about this book but also about other ones you've enjoyed, so you can continue to enjoy books by your favourite authors for years to come.

Dreams are meant to be lived,

Avril.

About The Author

Avril is an Australian author who lives with her family on acreage in South East Queensland. She writes mostly young adult and children's speculative fiction, but has been known to dabble in other genres. You can find more information about her at www.avrilsabine.com where you can also subscribe to her newsletter to be kept informed about new releases, current projects, blog posts and exclusive news.

Titles By Avril Sabine

Stories about strong characters and characters who discover their strengths.

SERIES

Assassins Of The Dead- Young Adult Fantasy/ Paranormal

Book 1: Dark Blade

Book 2: Dragon Touched

Book 3: Society Against Vampires

Book 4: King's Request

Dragon Blood- Young Adult Urban Fantasy (with elements of romance)

(5 book series)

Book 1: Pliethin

Book 2: Wyvern

Book 3: Surety

Book 4: Knight

Book 5: Mage

Dragon Mage- Young Adult Urban Fantasy (with elements of romance)

(Series two of Dragon Blood series)

Book 1: Promise

Dragon Blood Chronicles- Young Adult Urban Fantasy (with elements of romance)

(Companion stand alone series to Dragon Blood)

Book 1: Oath

Book 2: Betrayed

Guardians Of The Round Table- Young Adult Fantasy LitRPG

(Co-written with Storm and Rhys Petersen)

Book 1: Dexterity Fail

Book 2: Goblin Boots

Book 3: Singed Feathers

Book 4: Frog Mage

Book 5: Crystal Mine

Book 6: Cursed Harp

Rosie's Rangers- Young Adult Western Steampunk

(6 book series)

Book 1: Justice

Book 2: Vengeance

Book 3: Treachery

Book 4: Accused

Book 5: Wanted

Book 6: Corruption

Mark Of Kings- Children's Fantasy

(Upper middle grade/preteen)

(4 book series)

Book 1: The Arena

Book 2: The Island

Book 3: The Assassin

Book 4: The King

STAND ALONE SERIES

Demon Hunters- Young Adult Urban Fantasy/ Horror (with elements of romance)

Book 1: Blood Sacrifice

Book 2: Retribution

Book 3: Tainted

Book 4: Premonition

Book 5: Cursed

Book 6: Feud

Book 7: Extrication

Plea Of The Damned- Young Adult Urban Fantasy/Paranormal

(6 book series)

Book 1: Forgive Me Lucy

Book 2: Forgive Me Aiden

Book 3: Forgive Me Jena

Book 4: Forgive Me Kobe

Book 5: Forgive Me Marti

Book 6: Forgive Me Dawson

Realms Of The Fae- Young Adult Urban Fantasy (with elements of romance)

The Sword (short story in Like A Girl Anthology)

Heart Of Stone

Book 1: A Debt Owed

Book 2: Marked By The Hunt

Book 3: The Magic Collector

Book 4: An Unexpected Betrayal

Book 5: Imprisoned By Iron

Fairytales Retold (Short Stories)

Snow-White And Rose-Red

The Twelve Brothers

The Light Princess

Beauty And The Beast

Sleeping Beauty

Aschenputtel

The Golden Bird

The Frog Prince

The Death Of Koshchei The Deathless

Myths And Legends Retold (Short Stories)

Ion, Son Of Apollo

Sir Gawain And The Maid With The Narrow Sleeves

Princess Ilse, The Giant's Daughter

YOUNG ADULT NOVELS

Young Adult Fantasy (with elements of romance)

Elf Sight

Earth Bound

Young Adult Urban Fantasy

Stone Warrior (with elements of romance)

The Jungle Inside

Young Adult Contemporary (with elements of romance)

Through Your Eyes

The Ugly Stepsister

Perfect Little Princess

Young Adult Contemporary/Paranormal

Whispers In The Dark (with elements of romance and same sex relationships)

Over Too Soon (with elements of romance)

Young Adult Sci-Fi

Experiment X-One-Six (Urban Sci-Fi/Superheroes)

An Endless Dawn (Post Apocalyptic Sci-Fi)

CHILDREN'S BOOKS

Dragon Lord (Preteen/early teens) (Fantasy)

The Irish Wizard (Upper middle grade) (Urban Fantasy)

SHORT STORIES

Urban Fantasy

Eternally Late

Dealings With Joe

Glimpses (short story in That Moment When Anthology)

Contemporary

The Brat Next Door

Fantasy LitRPG

(Set in the same world as Guardians Of The Round Table Series)

Tales Of Inadon 1: The Disc (Co-written with Storm and Rhys Petersen) (short story in Game On! Anthology)

Post Apocalyptic Sci-Fi

Compulsive Directive

NONFICTION

A Year Of Weekly Writing Exercises (Creative Writing)

Cooking For Families With Allergies (Cooking) (Co-written with Storm Petersen)

Tell Me A Story, Grandma (Memoir)

For the most up to date details on available titles visit:

www.avrilsabine.com/books/bibliography

Plea Of The Damned Series

To learn more about this series visit:

www.avrilsabine.com/series/potd

BOOKS AVAILABLE IN THE PLEA OF THE DAMNED SERIES:

Book 1: Forgive Me Lucy

Book 2: Forgive Me Aiden

Book 3: Forgive Me Jena

Book 4: Forgive Me Kobe

Book 5: Forgive Me Marti

Book 6: Forgive Me Dawson

Disclaimer

This is a work of fiction. Names, characters, businesses, places, events and incidents are either the products of the author's imagination or used in a fictitious manner. Any resemblance to actual persons, living or dead, or actual events is purely coincidental. The opinions expressed or beliefs held are those of the characters and should not be assumed to be the opinions or beliefs of the author.